SERENDIPITY

written by: Stephen Cosgrove
illustrated by: Robin James

A Serendipity Book

Copyright © 1974 by Price/Stern/Sloan Publishers, Inc.
Printed in the United States of America. All rights reserved.

No part of this book may be reproduced in any form without written
permission from the publisher, except for brief passages included in
a review appearing in a newspaper or magazine.

Serendipity:
The Gift of Finding
Valuables or Riches
Not Sought.
(Webster)

On an iceberg far south in the Antarctic sat an egg. It was no ordinary egg, for it was four feet wide and eight feet tall and had a distinct pink shade to it.

Nobody knew what it was. The penguins and seagulls that lived on the iceberg just assumed that it had been there for a long time. And it probably had.

For years and years the egg sat there stuck in the ice, but then the iceberg began floating north.

The days became warmer. Finally the penguins and the seagulls all packed and went back to the Antarctic because they liked it cold.

The egg was left alone on an iceberg that was slowly melting.

One day, a curious thing began to happen.
The egg that had sat for so many years in the
ice twisted and squirmed, crickled and cracked,
and finally hatched.

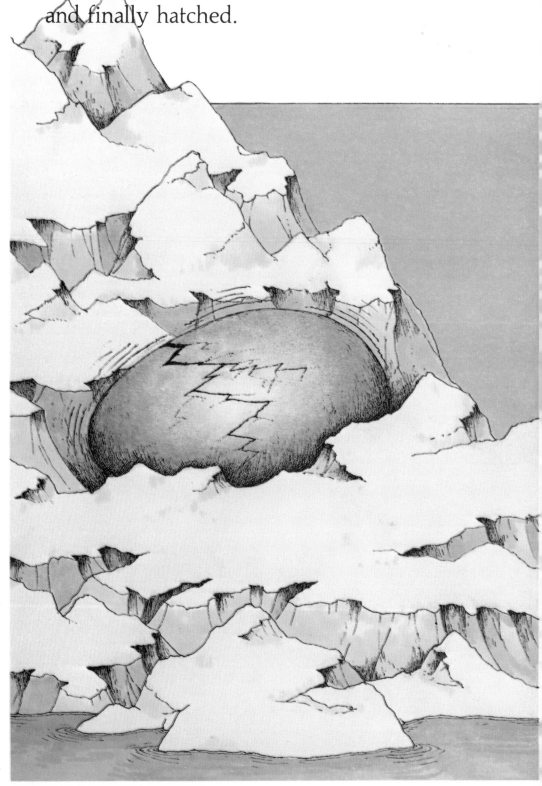

There, standing on wobbly legs and blinking her eyes in the bright sunshine, was…heaven knows what! She was big, pink and scared. I guess, for all practical purposes you could call her a sea serpent, though she really wasn't.

She stood there for a while just looking at everything there was to see. Suddenly the iceberg rolled with a large wave, and she slipped and slid right into the water.

She began floundering about, trying desperately to stay afloat. But since she had just hatched, she didn't know how to swim. She was making so much racket with her splashing and thrashing that a big, fat walrus swam over to see what all the commotion was about.

"Who—or what—are you?" asked the walrus.

"I don't know who or what I am!" she cried. And with that she flipped herself upside down. She would have drowned right there had not the walrus held her afloat. As quickly as he could, the big, fat walrus taught her how to swim.

"Well," said the walrus, "now that you've calmed down a bit, let's see if we can figure out just who you are!" He slowly swam around her, for she was growing even as he was talking. "Hmmmm...You're too big to be a tuna and too small to be a whale. You have no feathers, so you can't be a bird. I just don't know what you are."

She began to cry and cry. "I must be somebody. Why, I don't even have a name!"

"I may not be able to figure out who or what you are, but I surely can give you a name," said the walrus. "From now on you shall be called—hmmmm...Serendipity. And as you cannot stay here all alone, you will come with me, for I am on my way to the Island of Capri, where all the fishes of all the world are to meet. Possibly they can decide what you are and what you are to do."

Since Serendipity had nowhere else to go, she set out with the walrus for the Island of Capri.

They swam and swam into the warmer waters of the Atlantic Ocean. Every day Serendipity grew just a little bigger, until the walrus was constantly swimming in her shadow.

One day, as they were hurrying on their way, they heard cries for help just over the horizon. The two of them quickly swam to investigate.

There, right before them, was an aging dolphin trapped in a floating net.

"How did you get caught in that net?" asked Serendipity.

"I was swimming to the Island of Capri," said the dolphin, "when a fisherman threw this net upon me. Now he has gone for help to load me into his boat."

Serendipity turned to the walrus. "Should we try to help the old dolphin or should we hurry on our way?"

"Always help where you can, Serendipity," said the walrus, "and as your name suggests, you will always find valuable things you are not looking for."

Serendipity agreed, and she and the walrus set about trying to free the dolphin. But while they were busy at their task, the fisherman and his friend came back to their net.

"What are you doing there?" shouted the fisherman. "Get away from my net!" And with that he started to throw a large harpoon at the walrus, who was cutting the net with his tusks.

Without thinking of her own safety, Serendipity swam over to the boat. With a mighty heave, she flipped it over, throwing the fishermen into the water.

The fishermen were sputtering in the water, so Serendipity very carefully lifted them up and dropped them on the overturned boat where they hung on for dear life.

In the meantime, the walrus had freed the old dolphin, and the three of them swam quickly away.

"I am indebted to you," said the dolphin as they rested for a moment, "for saving me from the fishermen."

The dolphin looked at Serendipity for a moment and said, "I know the walrus, for he is a cousin of mine, but the likes of you I've never seen."

"I don't know who or what I am," she said. "But the walrus is taking me to the Island of Capri, where all the fishes of all the world are meeting. They will decide what I should do."

"I, too, am on my way to Capri," said the dolphin. "But we must hurry, for we have a long journey and very little time."

So once again Serendipity, the walrus, and now the dolphin set out for the Island of Capri.

They had swum for over two days when suddenly the water began to turn dirty and brown. Paper cups and bottles bobbed in the sea around them. The farther they swam, the more garbage there seemed to be, and the oil floated freely on the top of the water.

"What is all this?" asked Serendipity.

"Unfortunately," said the dolphin, "we must swim close to the land on our journey, and the land dwellers throw their garbage into the sea."

By this time they were unable to move at all because of all the garbage and junk floating on the water.

"Would it not be wise to dive low and swim away from all this?" asked Serendipity. She looked a little silly, for she had a banana stuck on her nose.

"No," said the walrus. "Running away won't help the water or the fish that swim in it."

Serendipity, over the past few days, had grown bigger and bigger, till now she towered over the walrus and the dolphin. Because she was so big, she had more garbage and oil on her than the other two put together. To rid herself of all that dirt and grime, she began bobbing up and down in the water. By doing so she created large waves that rolled onto the shore.

Finally, as she took one last dunk, she made such a large wave that it carried all the oil, all the garbage, and all that junk and threw it right up on the shore and on top of all the land dwellers who had thrown it into the sea to begin with.

The dolphin and the walrus laughed and cheered to see all that garbage leave the sea. "Oh, Serendipity," chuckled the walrus, "I'm sure the land dwellers will think very hard before they throw garbage into the sea again."

With the way clear before them, the walrus, the dolphin, and a proud Serendipity once again set off for the Island of Capri.

After a long and tiring journey, they finally arrived at the Island of Capri. There they found all the fishes of all the world. It was quite a sight to see. There were giant whales, tiny shrimp, chunky tunas and slippery salmon, just to name a few.

"We must leave you now," said the walrus and the dolphin, "for we have much to do." And with that they swam away from Serendipity into the milling crowds of fish.

"Well," thought Serendipity, "I am never going to find out who or what I am by staying here. I must move to the front and ask the leaders of all the fishes."

She bumped and pushed her way to the front, and there, to her surprise, was the fat walrus and the old dolphin.

"What are you doing here?" she asked.

"We are the leaders of all the fishes," they answered.

"But why hadn't you told me before? I have come all this way only to find that you were the ones who would tell me who or what I am!" she cried.

"Serendipity," said the dolphin, "we encountered many dangers on our trip here, and you overcame all of them. In doing so you have discovered that you are brave and kind, and that is what you are."

"As to who you are," said the walrus, "you are Serendipity, and like your name, you always gained riches that you did not seek."

"That is all well and good," said Serendipity, "But now that I know who and what I am, what am I to do?"

"As you are now the largest of all the fishes of all the world," said the walrus and the dolphin, "we hereby proclaim that you shall be the guardian of all the seas. It shall be your duty to protect the waters of the world from the land dwellers and to make sure that the oceans stay clear and blue."

If you ever
Throw your garbage
In the ocean,
Lake or sea
You'd better start
To rowing
For there will be…
Serendipity.